Ablaze

Kit Kyndall

Published by Amourisa Press, 2017.

Ablaze

Kit Kyndall

Amourisa Press and Kit Tunstall, writing as Kit Kyndall, reserve all rights to ABLAZE. This work may not be shared or reproduced in any fashion without permission of the publisher and/or author. Any resemblance to any person, living or dead, is purely coincidental.

© Kit Tunstall, 2015

(Previously published by Ellora's Cave from 2004 to 2014.)

Cover Images: Depositphotos.com

Join Kit's Mailing List[1] (www.kittunstall.com/newsletter) to receive notification of new releases and access bonus chapters for your favorite books. You get free books just for signing up! If you prefer to receive notifications for just one, or a few, of Kit's pen names, you'll have the option to select which lists to subscribe to at signup.

---

1. http://kittunstall.com/newsletter/

Chapter One

B lack smoke billowed down the hallway, obscuring Nick's view through his face shield. His peripheral vision tracked two teenagers in the Westbridge Academy's conservative uniforms hurrying toward the exit, clutching hands and sobbing. He thought about stopping the girls to ask if they had seen anyone else left in the building, but the air of panic surrounding them indicated they wouldn't be responsive.

Seeing they required no assistance, he and his partner moved on, Paula taking the lead. As they progressed down the hallway, the smoke thickened, settling lower to the floor. He reached for his SCBA automatically as they checked each classroom, quickly but methodically.

At the last room in the hallway, where the fire had originated, Nick and Paula stepped inside, dropping to a crouch as they moved through the room, searching for anyone remaining. His low vantage point allowed him to avoid the thickest concentration of the acrid smoke and improved his visibility.

The room appeared to be a science lab containing several long black tables with three chairs at each. All of the tables were bare of the clutter of academic paraphernalia, indicating either everyone had grabbed their belongings, or no one had been in the room when the fire started.

Under that assumption, he didn't expect to find anyone but indicated with a hand signal to Paula that he was checking the adjoining lab, as procedure dictated. With Paula behind him, he entered the second room, and his heart stuttered when he saw someone lying facedown on the floor in the corner. Nick moved closer at a rapid pace, identifying the form of a woman when he knelt beside her.

As Paula joined him, he rolled the woman onto her back and lifted her in his arms, not taking time to check her vitals. She settled over his shoulder easily. The woman was a negligent burden on his way from the building, and he emerged into fresh air seconds later, his partner close on his heels. Paula broke off to rejoin the group of firefighters gathered round the engine.

Nick went straight to one of the ambulances, where an EMT waited to care for her. He lowered the woman onto a waiting stretcher and stripped off his SCBA then pushed back his face shield, preparing to find his chief to inform him the building was clear. Nick's eyes fell on the face of the woman, and he caught his breath. Even the black smudges couldn't disguise her finely honed features. With olive skin and dark brown hair, she was a striking contrast to the crisp white sheet and pillow on the gurney.

Her eyes opened as the EMT slipped an oxygen mask over her face. The rich brown color reminded Nick of pools of molten chocolate. The bewilderment in them made his heart ache. Without removing his elkskin gloves, he took her hand and squeezed gently. "Everything's going to be fine, ma'am."

For a long second, her gaze didn't waver from his. Nick had the sensation she was peering into his soul. He squirmed at the thought, breaking eye contact when he caught sight of the chief. It was a struggle to release the woman's hand, much to his surprise. Glancing down once more, he saw her eyes had closed again. The sound of her harsh coughing remained with him as he made his way to Brady, the chief. Her frightened eyes haunted him, and it took all his willpower to push away thoughts of her and return to the business at hand. Never had he experienced such a connection in such a way, and the woman's image stayed with him as he rejoined the rest of the crew extinguishing the fire.

BREATHING HURT. COUGHING hurt even more, but Miri couldn't stifle the urge. The oxygen provided some relief from the burning, acrid sensation in her throat and lungs but didn't repress the reflex to clear the congestion. She was vaguely aware of the EMT hovering beside her, monitoring her vitals every few minutes, but couldn't manage to converse yet. Her throat was too raw. Even the thought of speaking made her wince.

The approach of a firefighter, stripped of his Nomex jacket, with a white T-shirt and red Nomex pants, distracted her temporarily from her misery. Miri's eyes widened when she recognized the black-haired, blue-eyed hunk as the man who had carried her from the building. Her stomach clenched with nerves—or the urge to vomit after a prolonged coughing fit—as he approached, a smile displaying his firm lips, set in a tanned face, to their best advantage.

He tapped the EMT on the arm. "How's she doing, Manny?"

"Pretty well." He pointed to the pulse oximeter attached to Miri's finger. "Her oxygen is ninety-eight."

"Will you be taking her to the hospital?"

Miri moved the oxygen mask. "No." She hardly recognized the hoarse voice emerging from her throat.

He turned his attention to her. "How're you feeling, ma'am?"

"Thirsty."

"I can take care of that."

She watched him walk away from her, heading toward the red engine emblazoned with PHFD on the side in black letters. The loose fit of his pants hid his buttocks and legs, but the T-shirt clung to his defined arms like a lover, revealing each bulge and flex.

When he returned, water bottle in hand, Miri quickly dropped her eyes to hide the fact she had been staring. The instant attraction to her rescuer disturbed her. She wasn't the type to have her head turned so quickly, and definitely not just by physical attributes. She tried telling herself gratitude was the only thing she felt for the man, but knew it wasn't true.

"Here you are, Ms.—" He unscrewed the cap before handing her the bottle.

"Zorga. Miriam Zorga." She handed the mask to Manny, nodding to acknowledge his cautionary words of sipping slowly, and took a small taste. The water was like Heaven, though tainted by the flavor of smoke lingering in her mouth. After two more small sips, she looked up at the firefighter. "Thank you for the water…and for saving my life."

He inclined his head. "That's my job."

"Still, I want to repay you. May I buy you dinner Friday night?" Miri's eyes widened at the invitation. What was she thinking? She never dated a man unless she had known him for a decent length of time, knew his character, friends, interests and flaws. She did not go out with men she had just met, no matter how sexy. She certainly wasn't the one to issue the request. A retraction hovered on the tip of her tongue, but his reply cut it off.

"It's not every day a beautiful woman offers me dinner. How can I say no?" His blue eyes sparkled, as if he sensed she had been about to withdraw the invitation.

She couldn't graciously change her mind now. Miri forced a small smile. "Does Poplin Hills Country Club suit you?"

"If that's what you want." The idea didn't seem to thrill him. "I'll pick you up if you'll give me your address."

"No." She winced at the panic in her tone, hoping the lingering huskiness masked it. "We'll meet there. Seven-thirty?" She held her breath, expecting him to argue. Hoping he would, giving her an out from the evening. She wouldn't feel at all guilty for rescinding the invitation should he prove to be forceful or controlling. To her disappointment, he simply nodded.

"I'll see you then." He started to turn but paused, looking down at her. "I'm Nick Martin, by the way." Then he was gone, fading back into the chaos of the scene on the front lawn of the staid private girls' school.

She blushed upon realizing she hadn't even caught his name before asking him to dinner. Hormones were to blame for her spontaneous action, which alarmed her further. She hadn't surrendered to the pull of hormones as a teenager. *It's about time you did,* whispered a sly voice in her mind—the voice she was careful to always repress and tune out. This time, it refused to be ignored, whispering all sorts of erotic suggestions about how the dinner date with Nick might end. Much to her surprise, she didn't want to ignore the voice this time.

MIRI GROANED AT THE sight in the mirror. Her attempt at sexy had ended up closer to disheveled. Thick hair hung around her face in a tangled mass, refusing to lie sleek, as she had envisioned. The black silk pants she hadn't worn for years reminded her why she hadn't worn them with the way they clung to her thighs, accentuating the cellulite she hid under skirts and looser slacks. The red shirt dipped too low, exposing what should have been generous cleavage on a different woman, but merely accented what she lacked.

Miri glanced at the clock, biting her lip. She had twenty minutes until she was supposed to meet Nick. Availing herself of valet parking would give her five extra minutes to fix the disastrous sight she currently presented. In record time, she stripped off the slacks and shirt, standing before the mirror in plain beige panties and a simple bra, grabbing her hair and pulling it back. Her hands were adept at forming the bun she wore every day, so that took little time. She secured it with pins and turned to her wardrobe, once again examining her available clothing. Everything seemed wrong, which had already led her to the two sexiest pieces she owned, and look how they had turned out.

With a sigh, she selected an A-line brown skirt and camel turtleneck sweater with subtle threads of gold woven throughout. Adding gold hoops and a pearl necklace made the outfit dressy enough for the country club, though boring. She chose to look on the bright side as she scooped up a gold clutch and hurried from her small house. Boring was sure to be a turnoff to the all-male Nick Martin, who must be accustomed to dating beautiful women. If he had no interest in her, that saved her the effort of fighting her attraction to him. The thought provided little consolation as she pushed her beige Saab four miles over the speed limit through the sparsely populated streets of Poplin Hills.

SHE ARRIVED FIVE MINUTES late, to find Nick sitting at the bar, watching for her. She nodded to the maître d' on her way through the spacious entryway, sparing no time to admire the antique teak wood, gold accents and deep red carpeting. The surroundings were familiar to her.

As she approached, Nick eased off his barstool, drink in hand. He tugged at the tie around his neck, as if unaccustomed to such accoutrements. With a critical eye, Miri examined him, noting he was sexy in the black suit but obviously uncomfortable. Her choice of restaurants was clearly a failure.

"I'm so sorry I'm not on time," she said in a rush when reaching him. "I'm never late…" She trailed off, deciding not to elaborate on why she was tardy.

He shrugged. "Don't worry. The beer is cold, and this is a nice place to wait." His expression betrayed the small white lie. Miri bit back a gasp at the electricity flaring between them when he took her hand. "All that matters is you showed up."

She cleared her throat, resisting the urge to tug her hand from his. The contact discomfited her. Not because he was a stranger, but because she liked it too much. "Are you ready for dinner?"

He nodded as the maître d' appeared at their side, as if psychically summoned. Nick didn't release her hand while they followed the man to a round table draped with a red tablecloth. Gold candleholders shone in the muted illumination from the crystal chandelier above the table. The flames from the red candles provided a cozy glow to accentuate the overhead lighting.

She breathed a sigh of relief when he had to let go of her hand as she prepared to sit at the table. The lightheadedness his touch had inspired almost faded, though she still felt giddy. Inner alarms screamed warnings about his effect on her, but Miri tried to ignore them as Nick pulled out her chair and seated her. Once again, his touch made her breathless.

Awkward silence fell between them as the maître d' departed after promising their server's attention shortly. She stared across the table, struggling not to stare into his sinfully blue eyes while trying to avoid the appearance of rudeness by ducking his gaze. She couldn't strike a balance and ended up looking away.

"Do you come here often?" His mood was difficult to discern. He didn't seem nervous, merely out of his element. Nick's voice didn't betray anything other than mild curiosity.

She nodded. "I have a lifetime membership." Miri didn't share the complete history of how it came to her. Her mother's numerous sordid marriages weren't a topic for first- date discussion. "It was a gift from my stepfather. He owned Poplin Hills Country Club a few years ago." Stepfather number four, to be precise, and the only one she had ever loved as a father.

His brow furrowed. "Richard Grazier was your stepfather?"

She nodded, struggling to maintain an indifferent façade as she studied him subtly, searching for a hint of avarice. More than once, she had disappointed a suitor who thought her stepfather had left her a large inheritance. His death had been several years after the divorce, and Miri had refused to accept anything from him other than companionship at that point. His other children and current wife had been relieved.

"It was hard on the town when Mr. Grazier passed. Everyone loved him."

Her heart softened at his sympathetic tone, and she struggled to make an intelligent response while hiding the tears in her voice. Thankfully, the arrival of the waiter prevented a reply, allowing her a minute to compose herself as Nick ordered a steak. Her order of grilled tilapia came automatically, and the server moved away.

The sommelier arrived within seconds, handing the wine menu to Nick. "What will you have this evening, sir?"

Miri almost grinned at his deer-in-the-headlight look. It was clear he wasn't a wine aficionado. Smothering her mirth, she said, "I don't believe we'll need a bottle tonight, Jules. Would you please bring me a glass of Sauvignon blanc?"

Jules turned to Nick. "For you, sir?"

"Beer's fine." Nick seemed unbothered by the wrinkling of the sommelier's brow as he left the table.

Again, the conversation lapsed. Miri asked a few meaningless questions, as did he, while accomplishing nothing but killing time. Out of desperation, she asked about his family. That was a topic she rarely broached with a stranger, for fear of having to give reciprocal information, but something needed to move along their exchange.

His posture relaxed, and he began telling her about his large family, all currently living in Boston.

As Nick spoke of his relations, Miri tried not to let envy plague her. As she laughed along with him at his shared remembrances, she couldn't help contrasting his childhood to hers. Nick's had been full of family and love, while hers was one long stretch of loneliness, with no siblings to share the trauma of uncles and stepfathers constantly coming and going, and a mother who was more concerned about her sex life than her daughter's welfare.

As their meal arrived, she asked, "Why are you in Oregon if your family is in Boston?"

"I wanted to see something besides Boston. I ended up here after traveling a few years." He shook his head. "It's funny. I thought I wanted to break away from the family traditions, but I ended up a firefighter just like my brothers and father, in spite of myself. It just took me a few years longer."

Her eyes widened. "Everyone in your family is a firefighter?"

"Just about." Pride shone in his eyes. Before she could ask anything else, his expression dimmed. "My oldest brother isn't a firefighter now. He married a woman who hated the whole idea, so he gave it up." It was clear what Nick would do in a similar situation. Miri would hate to be the woman who might ask him to give up his career.

As they ate, they managed to fill the meal with stilted, meaningless conversation. By dessert, Miri had marked up the date as a disaster and was admonishing herself about rash behavior when the bill arrived.

After settling the check, Miri rose to her feet, not waiting for Nick to pull out her chair. He rose just after her, putting his hand on her lower back as they left the restaurant. She searched for a painless way to close the evening, while getting across the point that she didn't want a repeat. It probably wasn't a concern. What man would want a second date with her after this calamity?

Outside, she handed a slip to the valet, noticing Nick didn't. They stood in silence as the young woman brought forth her Saab. At the curb, Miri turned to him, extending her hand. "Thank you for allowing me to repay you for saving me, Nick."

His lips twitched, as if repressing laughter. "My pleasure, Miri." He took her hand, caressing the palm with small circles of his thumb.

With a decisive nod, she pulled her hand from his and slid inside through the opened car door. Miri looked up at him, trying not to let her eagerness to escape show. "Well...good night."

He nodded but made no effort to walk toward his own car, wherever it might be. She waited for him to speak or move, so she could close the door and drive away, but he just stood there. "Good night," she said again, allowing a hint of exasperation to show.

"I'll follow you home to make sure you get there safely." "There's no need—"

He tapped on her windshield, already setting off in the direction of the self-parking area. "I'll catch up with you," he called over his shoulder.

She gritted her teeth and resisted the urge to run over him as he stepped in front of her car. No, she didn't want to dent the pristine grill, and blood would never come out of the beige paint.

As he jogged away, she slammed the door and shifted into drive, hitting the accelerator with a vengeance. All the way to her quiet home, she seethed with anger at his high-handedness. If he was pulling this stunt to get her to invite him in, he was in for a disappointment. Yes, he was too sexy for words, but she didn't like his attitude. He was too blunt for her tastes. She had cultivated a sophisticated life, courtesy of the time she had spent as Richard's stepdaughter. Nick would never fit into her existence. She couldn't even imagine him in her immaculate brick home, decorated in neutral colors with pastel accents.

She squirmed as an unwanted mental image came to her, of Nick sprawled across her periwinkle Egyptian-cotton sheets, with his hair tousled, his chest gleaming with sweat and the flush of passion still in his cheeks. Okay, there was one place he would complement her décor, but she refused to let her self-control slip enough to allow him into her home, much less the bedroom.

Chapter Two

By the time Miri parked in her garage, Nick's red Dodge Ram had caught up with her. He stopped at her curb, bounding out without invitation, to meet her at the door leading into the kitchen.

She pasted on a cool smile, valiantly ignoring the pool of heat that formed in her stomach when he touched her arm. "Thank you for the escort. It was unnecessary but appreciated."

He chuckled. "You don't lie well, Miri."

A blush swept through her cheeks. "Pardon?"

"You don't appreciate my chivalry. You're too busy trying to figure out what my angle is." He lifted an arm, resting his palm on the door behind her and bringing himself much closer.

Her spine stiffened. "You're mistaken, Mr. Martin. If you'll excuse me, I'm tired."

"Liar." His breath brushed her cheek. "You're thrumming with need. How long has it been since a man touched you here..." He brushed a hand across her hip. "Or here..."

His hand moved higher to cup her stomach before inching up to just below her breast. "Or here?"

Breathlessness made it difficult to speak. "I...I'll scream..."

"No, you won't, because you want this. You wanted it from the moment you saw me." Nick leaned closer still, his lips brushing against her cheek. "Want to know how I know?"

She thought she shook her head but couldn't be certain. Every nerve in her body responded to his touch, and her brain couldn't seem to coordinate movements.

"It was the same for me." His voice lowered an octave. "From the moment I looked into your eyes, it was like a fist in the gut. I've thought about you all week."

Miri summoned a reserve of mental clarity. "I haven't thought about you at all. I want you to go now, or I'll have to call the police."

He ignored her, leaning closer still, almost touching her lips with his. "You want me. Why fight it?"

"How can I want you after that disaster of a date? We have nothing in common." She chewed her lower lip, finding it difficult to concentrate with his proximity. "We could never have anything besides a physical connection."

"We have sex in common. Why does it have to be more complicated than that?" He kissed her then, just for a second, but it was long enough to melt her insides. "I don't want a relationship. I saw what love did to my brother. That's the last thing I want."

Finally, they had something other than the physical in common. "I don't want to fall in love either." After seeing the way her mother moved from lover to lover so casually, Miri had decided at a young age she would rather be alone than have a string of affairs. She had maintained her resolve to avoid relationships, never meeting a man worth compromising for.

But it had been so long since a man had held her. Her last lover had been a memory for three years now, cast aside because he wanted a deeper emotional commitment than she would give.

"Great. We know what we want from this. What's the harm?"

She shivered at his breath against her lips. "I don't have one-night stands."

"How about two nights...or a week?" His husky laugh danced along her nerve endings, exciting them to a fever pitch. "Take it one day at a time, and we'll move on when we're no longer hot for each other."

She stared into his eyes, swimming in the molten desire reflected there. Her brain said no, but her body softened against his, and Miri licked her lips. She cursed her weakness, even as she put a hand on his chest. "Do you want to come in?"

HE SWALLOWED UP THE space inside her home. Feng shui had failed in this instance. "You really like beige, don't you?"

Her neutral color scheme suddenly seemed boring next to Nick, and she had to resist the urge to hide the pastel pillows spread over the beige sofa. She owed him no excuses for her tasteful home, she reminded herself. "It's elegant."

Nick shrugged, dismissing the topic. "Coffee?"

She exhaled a breath she hadn't been aware of holding. It had been so long since a man had violated her sanctuary that she had forgotten how the process worked. Had she expected him to leap on her, take her on the floor and leave? Miri shook her head at the thought, squashing the ripple in the back of her mind that liked the scenario. "Of course. I have Seattle Sunrise or Mocha Mulberry."

His brow quirked. "Never mind. I'm strictly black, plain." "Your loss. May I offer you an iced tea?"

Nick scanned her apartment. "Do you have beer?" She shook her head. "I rarely drink at home." "Tea is fine."

She turned to the kitchen, leaving Nick to settle on the sofa. As she peered through the opened top of the Dutch door, she saw him tossing her cushions haphazardly in the corner. Miri gritted her teeth to avoid saying something. She wasn't fitting the man into her life. Simply her bed.

Her hands shook at the thought, and she slopped a bit of tea from the pitcher onto the floor when removing it from the fridge. With a smothered curse, she ripped a paper towel from the roll on the counter and cleaned up the spot.

The dispenser on the refrigerator hummed, but no ice dropped into the glass when she pressed it against the sensor pad. Frowning, she bent at the waist to examine the dispenser just as the ice burst free, exploding from the chute into the glass, on the floor and at Miri.

She slammed the glass onto the counter with more force than necessary and bent to pick up the cubes. How many more signs did she need to know this was a bad idea? What had she been thinking, agreeing to a fling with Nick Martin, a man she had known less than a week? She couldn't allow libido to overrule common sense. Once he had his tea, she would explain she had changed her mind and send him away.

With that decision made, Miri's hands steadied, and she was able to get another glass, fill it with ice and put it on the counter. Not a drop of tea spilled from the pitcher as she filled the glasses, and she grasped them firmly before returning to the living room.

Nick hadn't waited for an invitation to make himself comfortable. He'd kicked off his shoes, removed his jacket and tie and rolled up the sleeves of his light-blue shirt. His sock-covered feet screamed at her from their perch on her antique coffee table. She stared at them when putting his glass of tea on a coordinating coaster.

"Thanks." He patted the cushion beside him. "Sit with me."

She eyed the recliner and sat beside him with a soft sigh. Had he read her intentions to maintain distance between them?

Nick took the glass, gulping the tea in three long swallows. Miri watched his throat move, mesmerized by the cords flexing. Her mouth watered as she imagined trailing her tongue across his flesh.

To distract herself, she took a sip of tea and choked on it. Nick came to the rescue by patting her back, managing to knock the rest of the tea down the front of her sweater. She gasped as liquid soaked her front and then gasped again when Nick's bare hands brushed down her breasts in an effort to remove the ice cubes. She surrendered the glass to him, unable to speak for a moment.

"Come on. You need to get out of that. It's soaking wet." He took her hand, and Miri stood when he did, following him down the hall. "Which room?"

She opened her mouth to tell him he had done enough, that he should leave now, but a small, "The door at the end of the hall," issued from her. What? Why was she so timid, going along with this? She wasn't that horny, was she?

Her nipples hardened at that moment as heat pooled between her thighs when she ran into Nick's back. Her body reeled from the contact, forcing her mind to admit maybe she was that turned on. She wanted him more than any man who had ever been invited into her bedroom. Why was she fighting it?

He pushed open the door and stepped in ahead of her, whistling through his teeth. "Nice." His eyes were on the blonde sleigh bed, complete with a beige velvet comforter that invited stroking. "I may never leave, darlin'."

"Tonight only. We agreed."

Nick turned to her, wearing a wolfish grin. "Actually, we agreed for however long it lasts."

Had she agreed to that just by inviting him in? Miri lifted a shoulder, dismissing the disagreement. He might or might not agree, but they were on a night-by-night basis, with no guarantees.

"Let me help you with that. I'll bet that virgin wool is scratchy when wet."

Miri stepped away from him, hoping her cool expression hid the heat spiraling through her as her mind conjured up an entirely different use for virgin wool on wet places. "I can handle it."

"I know, but it's more fun if I do it." Nick cocked his head, winking. "C'mon."

She stood still, holding her arms loosely at her sides. The first feather-soft touch of his fingers at the waistband of her skirt made her stomach quiver. She sucked in a breath as he pulled the sweater slowly from the skirt, an inch at a time, until her waist was bared. He moved the sweater higher, revealing her stomach, which quaked continuously as his fingers stroked exposed areas.

"Your skin is so soft. Like silk. I can't wait to taste it." Nick spoke with an arrogant certainty that he would taste whatever he liked. She didn't contradict him, not wanting to. Now that she had given in to this insanity, she intended to enjoy it fully. What good were morning-after regrets without a helluva night before?

He pulled the sweater over her head, and Miri trembled at the hunger in his gaze. It made her feel vulnerable and desirable all at once. Had any man ever inspired such feelings before? Maybe her previous interludes had been so tepid because she knew all about the men selected to be lovers. There was mystery with Nick, heightening her anticipation. She didn't know what he would do next.

His lips twitched. "A beige bra too, Miri?" She shrugged. "I like beige."

His fingers unfastened the back clasp with confidence, letting the cups lower to just above her nipples. "You need some color in your life, darlin.'"

She shook her head but offered no further protest, too entranced by the way his fingers danced across the silk cups, easing them away from her small breasts with a finesse never equaled by any preceding him. Miri hardly noticed the bra as it dropped to the floor but didn't miss his fingers caressing her nipples. They hardened again, straining to meet his fingers, begging for attention. A mingled gasp-groan escaped her when he lightly pinched one. "Nick?"

He met her eyes. "Yes?" "Kiss me."

She had barely uttered the second word when his arms were around her and her body melted against his. Miri tilted her neck to meet his descending head, and their lips touched. She was almost surprised sparks didn't flare when their flesh met. His lips were firm and demanding but also giving. She molded hers to his, sighing at the electricity humming between them. How could a kiss be so earth shattering?

It only got better when he parted her lips with his and slid inside, playfully pushing his tongue against hers before slipping over the surface. Miri caught his tongue with hers, pinning it briefly before he broke away.

The kiss changed, getting deeper and more passionate. Nick's hands ventured from her back to her buttocks, cupping and squeezing them as he fitted her pelvis against his. His cock pressed insistently against her pussy, making her dizzy with need.

Nick's mouth moved from hers and took a leisurely trip across her cheek to her ear. Miri gasped when he twirled his tongue around the tiny hoop in her lobe, darting through the jewelry to lick a sensitive spot. She put her arms around his waist, pressing him closer. He breathed a short laugh into her ear before sucking the lobe and earring into his mouth to bite gently.

When he lifted his head, Miri surged forward, determined to see if his neck was as tempting as she had imagined. Nick jerked at the first stroke of her tongue down the column of his throat then groaned when she sucked skin between her teeth to nibble.

"Why do you scrape back your hair? I bet it's gorgeous."

She would have answered it was practical for work, but her mouth was too busy devouring his skin. He tasted sweet, with a hint of salt, and the woodsy fragrance of his cologne contributed to his allure. She didn't hesitate in her appointed task as he unwound her hair from the bun, letting the dark brown locks fall to the middle of her back.

"God, Miri, I could lose myself in here." Nick brought a handful to his face, rubbing the strands against his cheeks. "I can't wait to see you on the bed, with your hair spread out on the pillow."

"Umm." Miri kept kissing his neck while her fingers undid the buttons of his shirt to the waistband of his pants. After parting the lapels, she let her mouth venture lower, licking a path across his chest, keeping a hand there to touch the lightly furred skin, running her fingers through his chest hair as her tongue swept over his nipple, eliciting a moan. His hand tightened on her hair, dragging her closer, and Miri surrendered to instinct.

She swirled her tongue around his nipple in small circles, gradually increasing the radius while still stroking his chest with her hand. Her other hand hooked into his waistband and one finger was bold enough to slip inside to caress his waist.

She cried out with surprise when Nick swung her into his arms to carry her to the bed. He didn't bother to push back the velvet comforter to reveal the nine-hundred- count cotton sheets underneath. The velvet cradled her back as Nick's body hovered over her front. Her breasts fit perfectly against his chest as he aligned his body over hers. She wriggled, teasing her nipples with the hair on his torso. "You're wearing too many clothes."

He cupped the back of her head, bending her neck to take control of her mouth. "You too," he said, before touching his lips to hers. The kiss was slow, with each stroke of his tongue branding her as his. She was aware of the possessiveness in his actions and reveled in it but refused to focus on the implications of giving him more power in the liaison than she should.

He eased away from her long enough to strip off his shirt, remove his belt and unfasten his pants, leaving the zipper and button of his trousers open. Miri lifted her hips as he fumbled for the zipper at the back of the skirt, easing the passage of the garment.

Nick touched her thighs, stroking the bare flesh. "I didn't figure you for a garter belt girl."

She squirmed as he ran a thumb over the beige garter belt before rubbing the silky hose on her thigh. Should she ruin the illusion and tell him she had resorted to an old- fashioned garter belt and thigh-highs because her last pair of pantyhose had ripped? No. "I need a surprise or two. Keeps things interesting."

"That it does." His hand moved higher, past the garter belt and bare skin, to her panties. They were beige too, but he made no comment.

Miri arched her hips when he ran his thumb down her slit, exciting every nerve centered there. Moisture accompanied the motion, and the panties seemed to chafe unbearably against her pussy.

Nick grew bolder, penetrating the elastic side of the panty to caress her pussy. "You're so wet."

"I want you." She was going to go insane if he didn't move along soon. She groaned as his thumb slipped inside her, probing her entrance. "Please."

"Not yet."

She gnashed her teeth when he pulled away again, this time to remove her panties. She reached for the clip on one of the garters, but his hand stayed hers. "I'll take care of it." Nick dispensed with the garter belt and panties quickly, leaving only the thigh- highs.

Miri lay there watching him, wondering what he planned next. Should she take the initiative? She wasn't shy, but there was something so manly about Nick that it precluded her feeling confident enough to demand what she wanted. He might have a dominant personality, but more importantly, he made her want to submit to his whims.

She reached out, running her hand up and down his bicep. "What do you want me to do?"

"Nothing. I just want to look at you." Nick nudged her thighs wider so he could kneel between them. His gaze never wavered from her pussy as he parted it with one hand. The cool air on heated flesh induced a shiver in Miri, and she held her breath, wondering if she would feel his tongue on her.

Instead, a finger from his other hand circled her clit slowly as he bent forward. His tongue rasped wetly across one of her swollen nipples, teasing her unbearably. He sucked the bud deeper into his mouth as his fingers mimicked the movement to plunge deep into her pussy. Miri arched her hips, straining for more of his hand.

Nick complied with her unspoken request by thrusting his fingers in and out of her while circling her clit with firm strokes. His tongue laved her nipple, and she squirmed under the passionate onslaught. She was so hungry for him, just aching everywhere. It no longer seemed foolish to rush into a fling. Now, she couldn't get there fast enough. "Please, Nick. I need you."

He lifted his head from her breast but took his time withdrawing from her pussy, stroking her for another minute before relenting. She was slick with need when he stood up to remove his pants. The sight of his thick cock flooded her pussy with moisture. Miri imagined stroking him, tracing her fingers down the throbbing veins of his shaft and caressing the mushroom head as it spasmed against her hand. She watched impatiently as he pulled a condom from his pocket to sheath his cock before returning to her.

Nick took up the same position between her thighs, stretching out atop her. He didn't allow his full weight to rest on her as his hand parted her pussy to guide his cock inside her. Miri cupped his buttocks, pulling his cock in as deeply as she could. Her body accepted the length of him with surprising ease considering how long it had been since she had taken a lover.

She arched her hips, meeting his first thrust. The pace was slow, inciting a surge of desire that built in ever-increasing pulses. Miri's nails formed half-moons in the flesh of his buttocks as he thrust in and out of her, met eagerly each time by her. Nick's hand slipped between their bodies, his thumb seeking out and stroking her clit in time with his thrusts.

His cock was deep inside her, seeking to learn every inch of her pussy while his fingers memorized her clit. Miri cried out when Nick buried his mouth against her neck to bite her with more vigor than tenderness. His roughness excited her, much to her surprise. She was used to polite lovemaking, not the uninhibited variety that Nick seemed so adroit at.

She closed her eyes, struggling to contain a cry of pleasure as her pussy contracted around him. Convulsions swept through her, emanating from deep in her womb and squeezing his cock to milk every last drop of satisfaction from him. The world looked fuzzy when viewed through the haze of passion obscuring her vision, and her breathing was heavy. It was difficult to draw in a deep breath as she hovered on the edge of coming, just before plunging forward. A cry escaped her as her body went rigid with release.

Spasms shook her, making her pussy contract even tighter around his cock, which spasmed in time with the tremors racking her body. Miri tried to drag him inside her by digging her nails even deeper into the skin of his buttocks as afterglow started the process of making her muscles relax.

He stiffened against her, thrusting frantically a couple of times before staying deep inside her. Nick seemed to make no effort to conceal his husky groan of fulfillment as he let loose his satisfaction. His cock released in spurts that filled her with contentment, renewing milder spasms inside her core. Their bodies shook in time with each other for what might have been seconds or hours, uniting them as one for that short time.

When it was over, he didn't withdraw from her. Nick turned on his side, bringing Miri with him, and tucking her body close to his. He brushed a kiss across her forehead, murmured, "Thank you," and held her.

How did she respond? She wanted to weep with the pleasure he had given her. Never had it been so good. What about Nick completely fulfilled her when no other man had?

As he slipped into sleep, emitting soft snores, Miri cautioned herself to be careful. Nick was dangerous to her ordered life and sheltered heart. If he could breach her body so easily, what could he do to her carefully controlled emotions?

Chapter Three

M iri awoke alone, finding a note and the slight indent his head had left on the pillow the only proof he had been there. That, and the minor aches of gratification. The twinges were more pronounced when she leaned forward to retrieve the note.

Sorry I can't be here when you wake up, but I had an appointment I couldn't cancel. Be ready at seven. We're doing things my way tonight.

Nick

She frowned at the note, questioning the veracity of his vague appointment. Had it been an excuse to leave, to avoid the awkward conversation that might have awaited him if he had been there when she awoke? His high-handed tone didn't please her either. How dare he issue a dictate? She should make plans with someone else tonight, to be gone when he came around. That would show him she wasn't at his disposal.

Miri knew she wouldn't stand him up as she climbed from the bed, ill-at-ease from her nakedness. The T-shirt she normally wore to bed lay over the beige armchair in the corner. For however long this fling lasted, the old T-shirt could stay there. He was too intoxicating to cut short this...whatever it was...prematurely.

Refreshed by the previous night, she strolled to the French doors and opened them, squinting as sunshine flooded the room. Still naked, she took a step onto her balcony to survey the neighborhood. It wasn't quite eight, but several neighbors were engaged in weekend chores as children played on the streets.

She leaned against the wooden rail, hugging her arms over her breasts, wondering what prompted her to stand outside in the nude. The others in her conservative, upwardly mobile neighborhood would be shocked if they looked up at her balcony and saw her like this. They'd be even more shocked, might even shun her, if they knew the local high school science teacher had spent all night in bed with a man she hardly knew.

A giggle escaped Miri, and she clapped her hand over her mouth, alarmed by the blithe sound. It brought a return to sanity, and she hurried inside, closing the French doors behind her. For a moment, she had been a free spirit, not unlike her mother Marnie. What was she thinking?

Last night's decision to end things with Nick at a one-night stand had been a good one. If she was going to be crazy enough to see him again, even for one more night, she had to keep a rein on her impulses, for fear that she become too much like her mother. Shaking her head with disgust at the very idea, Miri padded into the bathroom, intent on showering and slipping into clothes as soon as possible. Naïvely perhaps, she believed she could conceal the secret thoughts plaguing her mind simply by hiding her body under garments.

AGAINST HER BETTER judgment, she was waiting for Nick by six forty-five, pacing the house, pausing every few minutes to stare at the grandfather clock in the entryway, mutter under her breath and mentally chastise her foolishness once more.

Her internal cautions to be sensible did nothing to slow her racing heart when her doorbell rang at seven. With features schooled in a composed arrangement, Miri opened the door to Nick and forgot how to breathe. The black T-shirt hugged his arms and torso indecently, revealing every flex and bulge as he moved. The faded jeans, now a worn gray, clung to his legs like a second skin. Her hands itched to test the fabric to see if it was as soft as it appeared. She knew from experience that underneath she would find rock-hard flesh.

"You look delicious," he said, stepping over the threshold without waiting for her to issue an invitation. Nick leaned forward to kiss her, lightly stroking her lips with his tongue. Straightening, he towered over her again, so close she could feel his body heat.

She longed to melt against him but held herself erect by sheer willpower. "Thank you." Did he really consider this pale-yellow sheath delicious? Bought to wear to an Easter service she had planned to attend with an ex-lover, the dress had gone unused when they had split days before the holiday.

He nodded. "Too dressy though. Do you have jeans?" Before she could respond, he said, "Go change."

Miri glared at him. Now was the time to nip his bossiness in the bud. "Don't be so patronizing. I've been making my own decisions for a long time, so I don't need your input on my wardrobe."

Nick's eyes widened. "Sorry, darlin'. I meant nothing by it. I want you to be comfortable. Where we're going, jeans are the norm, but it's up to you."

Put like that, her anger faded. "I'll be right back." Miri returned to her room, half- expecting Nick to follow for a repeat performance of last night. To her disappointment, as she slipped on her sole pair of blue jeans, still stiff with newness, he never made an appearance. She deliberately loitered over selecting a top, hoping he would come in, but he didn't.

With a sigh of disgust at her actions, she chose a beige square-necked tunic made of a gauzy fabric, suggesting more than it truly showed, while simultaneously slipping her feet into loafers. When she found Nick in the living room, he whistled. She extended her arms, doing a complete circle. "Does this meet your approval?"

"You bet, darlin'." He stood up, putting an arm around her waist on the way to the door. His hand slipped inside her back pocket, and he winced. "Those jeans sure are stiff, unless your ass is that firm."

His words should have appalled her but instead she had to stifle a laugh. "They're new. I've only worn them once, on a field trip with the seniors last year."

He made no further comment as they left her house until Miri headed in the direction of her Saab. He tightened his grip on her pocket, steering her left, to a gleaming red motorcycle parked at the curb. "We'll take my Concours."

Miri was already shaking her head even as he continued to bring her with him across her front lawn. "I've never ridden one before."

"It's about time, don't you think?"

"No, I—"

He ignored her objections by thrusting a helmet into her hands. "Try this on for size, Miri."

"Nick, I'm not riding on this—" She gasped when he pushed the helmet on her head, squashing her bun.

He pushed up the face shield and leaned forward to steal a kiss. "Live a little." His eyes twinkled. "Unless you're scared?"

Hell, yes, she was scared, but not about to admit it. Miri firmed her trembling lips, nodded just once and cinched the strap of the helmet under her chin. "Let's go."

Nick's laugh was rich with joy and too contagious. She had to bite her tongue to keep from chuckling along with him. At least the moment of mirth tempered her nerves, and she was almost relaxed by the time Nick put on his helmet and directed her to sit on the seat behind him after he climbed on.

Her hands shook when she grasped his shoulders to steady herself while mounting the seat. The position was odd, and she clutched him tighter when he started the motorcycle. The Kawasaki seemed to roar like an injured beast, and she was two seconds from backing down from his challenge when he shifted into gear and took them onto the road.

Miri's eyes widened with shock when the vibrations of the seat transmitted to her pussy. Without thought, she shifted positions to feel more of the power, loosening her death grip on Nick's neck in the process.

She spared a glance for the road, deciding she didn't like the way the lines whipped by with nauseating quickness but otherwise enjoying the ride. It was difficult to remain in fear for her life when the engine's vibrations kept her constantly aroused, just shy of an orgasm.

Nick detoured from Main Street to an area of town she never frequented. If any place in Poplin Hills could be considered seedy, it was the strip of establishments on Route 7. Her apprehension grew when he slowed down the bike to turn into Hooch's, a local tavern with colorful clientele. She'd never been inside, but rumors abounded of drunken brawls, marriage-ending events and other horrors taking place there every night of the week. No decent citizen would step foot inside.

All those thoughts ran through her mind when Nick parked by the door beside a beaten-up black motorcycle, but she didn't utter a word when he helped her from the bike and removed her helmet. She had taciturnly agreed to let Nick set the rules for tonight. It was too late to argue now. She just hoped they survived the night without anyone connected to the school seeing her at Hooch's.

As Miri took a seat at a table shrouded by shadows in the corner of the room, she swore she could still feel the vibration of the engine through her body. Her damp pussy throbbed in time with her heart, seeking release. Would anyone notice if she pushed Nick down across the table and had her way with him right there? Surveying the dim interior, clouded with smoke, thick with partiers, she couldn't say with absolute certainty they would. It was the sort of place one could do just about anything without having the other patrons look askance.

"What would you like?"

"Chard...beer, please." When in Rome...

Miri's gaze remained on Nick's tight form as he moseyed up to the mahogany bar to place their orders. Her eyes narrowed when a blonde sitting on a stool gave him an enthusiastic greeting that included a wet kiss on the lips. Was she jealous of the bimbo? How could she be, considering she had no emotional ties to Nick?

Nonetheless, the sting of jealousy bit into her when the blonde climbed off the stool to plaster herself against Nick. Miri bunched her hands into fists atop her thighs, fighting the urge to march over and rip every bleached hair out of the slut's head.

Her strong reaction jarred Miri back to reality. She wasn't the kind of woman to get into a barroom brawl, especially over a man she had spent just one night with. Her anger switched to simmer as Nick brushed off the woman, got their drinks and returned to the table. She struggled to hide any hint of how she felt behind an aloof smile when he sat down.

"You didn't say tap or bottle, so I took a guess." He pushed a mug of draft beer across the scarred black table.

She lifted it, took an enthusiastic gulp and managed to hide a grimace of distaste. "Who was the woman at the bar?" Her frosty tone pleased her.

A hint of red might have tinged his cheeks. It was difficult to tell with the low lighting. "Um, a friend."

"You should have invited your friend to join us. I hate for her to be alone." Nick shifted, looking uncomfortable. "I'm sure Chloe won't be lonely long."

"Hmm." She took another sip of the beer, finding it easier to tolerate with each drink. "What do you do here, besides drink?"

"Dance, play pool." He shrugged. "Hang out."

She wasn't accustomed to hanging out. Miri liked plans for everything. She always knew which movie she was going to watch at the theater before going, always reserved activities well in advance when going on vacation and never changed her mind about anything at the last minute. Drumming her fingers on the table, she scanned the bar again, noticing one of the pool tables was free. "Teach me how to play pool." What she really wanted to do was request he take her home and fuck her until she forgot her own name, but held back. They were having a civilized fling, which included the pretense of dating.

"Sure. Go hold the table, and I'll get the balls from Belle."

Miri took her mug with her to the table and stood by it with a hand on the edge, not sure if she was holding it properly. This time, Nick picked a spot several stools down from Chloe as he conversed with the mid-forties woman behind the bar. Soon, he returned with pool balls.

As he racked them, he asked, "You've never played?"

"No." The closest she had come had been the times Marnie left her in the car while she went in to drink at various bars. Miri shuddered slightly, remembering the numerous nights she had fallen asleep in various old cars, waiting for her mother to stumble out at closing time. "It never appealed to me. Until now."

"Fair enough. I'll let you break." "Break?"

"Grab a cue and go to the other end of the table."

When Miri had selected a green cue from the wall and stood on the opposite end from Nick, he rolled a white ball to her. She had seen enough on television to know to chalk the cue. After finishing, she figured out where to put the ball and assumed breaking was the act of scattering the balls after he took away the rack holding them.

The cue was clumsy in her hands as she maneuvered it into position to hit the ball. Before she could make her shot, he moved behind her, standing so close she could feel his cock pressing into her buttocks. "Now what?" The breathless question sounded coy, not logical, as she had intended.

"Don't clench the cue so tightly." He put his hand over hers, loosening her grip while repositioning her hold. His other hand rested briefly on her hip before taking possession of her free hand, which he placed on the table, positioning it exactly. "Rest the cue here, but lightly. You want to be unrestrained when you shoot." He kept his hands over hers, demonstrating the way she should shoot. "Keep your motions fluid."

To her disappointment, Nick withdrew to let her make the shot. As soon as he stopped touching her, she forgot everything he had shown her. The cue barely touched the ball, sending it only a couple of inches off its straight course, without getting anywhere near the pyramid of balls at the other end of the table. She groaned, ready to quit.

"My turn." Nick took a cue and held it with confidence born of practice. Miri's eyes didn't stray as he leaned over the table to make his shot. The way his buttocks clenched in the tight jeans dried out her mouth. The beer she gulped did little to provide relief but kept her from uttering a moan when he completed his shot, making his body one streamlined work of art. The kind meant to be touched, not hung on a wall and admired from a distance.

The cue ball scattered the others when it slammed into their midst, causing three to drop into pockets immediately. He looked over his shoulder. "It's still my turn, but why don't you go ahead?"

She shook her head, in no hurry to end his turn. He was delicious enough to watch all night. "Play by the rules."

He started to walk past her but turned to pull her against him and press his mouth to hers. Miri's first thought was of protesting the public kiss. Her second was all about the kiss itself. She wrapped her free arm around his waist, trying to pull him closer. His mouth devoured hers as his tongue feathered against her lips.

When he pulled away, his grin was full of smug arrogance and a healthy dose of satisfaction. "Darlin', I've always found it more fun to break the rules." He moved past, leaving her with a lingering squeeze on her bottom.

The balls seemed to disappear with lightning speed as Nick set about putting them into the pockets. She watched with rapt attention each time his muscles bunched or flexed, studied his expression for clues of his mood and felt the moisture in her pussy spread. By the time he knocked the eight-ball into the corner pocket, a light sheen of perspiration misted her body and she was lightheaded with arousal.

"Another?" he asked, rounding up the balls from under the table, where they had dropped after going into the pockets.

She shook her head. "Where's the ladies' room?"

"Down the hall." He pointed to a sign across the room. "Are you sure? You didn't get to play much."

"It's fine." She abandoned her beer and rushed to the restroom, shaking with the effort not to make a fool of herself. Her body ached for his. She was hotter than she had ever been, dripping with need. A few minutes of privacy was all she needed to collect herself. She hoped.

The restroom was as dim as the rest of the bar but not as smoky. There were two stalls, and she chose the handicapped one because it was closer. Miri locked the door and leaned against it, taking deep breaths that did nothing to calm her. This night had been nothing but foreplay, and she was ready for the main event. The only thing that had stopped her from begging Nick to leave was she didn't think she could wait to get back to her place.

The main door opened, and she tried to halt her rapid breathing. Her inhalation turned to a gasp when Nick peeked over her stall. "What are you doing? This is the ladies' room."

He grinned, unrepentant. "Open up."

She shook her head, even as her fingers obeyed his command and turned the lock. A flutter of common sense had her reaching for the door as he swung it open. "You can't...we can't."

"Remember the rules, darlin'." Nick entered the stall with her, locking the door. He was too close for rational thought as he pinned her against the side of the stall, pressing his mouth to hers. "Break them," he said, right before kissing her.

Propriety dictated she push him away, but her body had other ideas. Miri clung to Nick, running her fingers through his hair with one hand while resting the other at his waist. A moan escaped her when Nick's hand slid under the hem of her tunic to caress her stomach. His tongue thrust inside her mouth, and she met it eagerly, parrying his attempts to explore all of her.

One of his hands moved higher, cupping her breast through her bra, while his thumb rubbed over her swollen nipple, inflaming it with the lacy fabric. She nipped his tongue, earning a pinch that served only to heighten her arousal. Her hips arched of their own accord, bringing her dripping pussy against his cock, separated only by the fabric of their jeans. The barrier was too much, and she wanted to strip off their clothes and have him pin her to the wall.

Nick broke the kiss to sweep his mouth down her throat, pausing to bite the bend of her neck with just enough pressure to elicit a moan. Miri tightened her fingers in his hair, trying to halt his descent as he slid lower. He ignored her temporary resistance, and she stopped fighting when he pushed her tunic above her breasts. His tongue swept into the valley of her cleavage, modest as it was, and he inhaled. "You smell like flowers," he said against her skin, sparking flicks of heat with every breathy word.

"You smell like sex." The blunt words shocked her, but he didn't seem taken aback by her uttering them. And it was true. Nick smelled, tasted, walked and talked S-E-X. She couldn't help but respond. Urgent hands tugged his T-shirt up so she could caress his abdomen, which fluttered under her hand. His cock pressed more insistently against her pussy through the jeans, and she parted her thighs wider to allow it to nestle deeper.

To her surprise, he shifted her suddenly, pressing her against the wall and supporting her on one of his thighs while she braced her hands on his shoulders. His movements were smooth and quick when he released the back clasp of her bra and pushed the cups above her breasts, along with the tunic. Once freed, her breasts strained for his touch, and Miri's nipples tingled with warmth.

Nick's mouth was gentle, but with a hint of roughness, when he took possession of one nipple. The bead disappeared into his mouth, where he flicked his tongue over the tip, causing her to stifle a cry of passion. Miri dug her nails into his shoulders, pulling him closer still while writhing against his thigh, seeking relief for the inferno blazing inside her pussy. "Nick, I can't take this." They had to leave, find the nearest bed and satiate each other.

He lifted his head to stare into her eyes. "Yeah, you can, darlin'. Trust me." Then his hands moved to her waistband, dispensing with the button and zipper to plunge his hand inside. His fingers stroked her pussy through the silky panties she wore, and Miri tossed her head from side to side, desperate for relief, as his fingers teased her clit through the silk. "Please, Nick. Let's get out of here."

"Easy." His hand left her pants, and he lowered her back to her feet. Miri experienced a dart of disappointment, despite it having been her request to stop and find somewhere else more private. Her discontent changed to confusion when Nick got on his knees before her.

Her eyes widened when he pulled down her jeans and panties. Somehow, she managed to remain coherent enough to kick off her loafers and step out of them.

There was no mistaking his intentions as he leaned forward, tongue extended. She twined a hand in his hair, not sure if she wanted to push him away or pull him closer. He didn't allow her to choose, lunging forward suddenly, tongue seeking out her heat. Miri closed her eyes with a gasp, leaning against the stall wall for support, as Nick's tongue sought out all her secret places, paying special attention to her clit, swollen with need.

The moist swipes of his tongue probing her opening made Miri ball her hands into fists to keep from shouting. Nick pressed his tongue deeper inside her pussy. She shifted with restless energy, needing more than his intimate kiss. She wanted him inside her.

Nick seemed to have read her thoughts, because he brought a hand between her thighs. His tongue abandoned her opening, leaving her temporarily bereft, until two of his fingers plunged inside to take its place. It wasn't his cock, but the digits were almost enough to satisfy her. When Nick swirled his tongue around her clit, she cried out while mindlessly thrusting against his face as spasms in her pussy built in intensity.

She was on the brink of release when the outer door opened. Miri's eyes snapped open, and she froze as footsteps went past their stall, though Nick continued to lick her pussy. She pulled on his hair, trying to get his attention, but he remained focused on his task. "Nick," she said so quietly she barely heard it herself as the door to the stall beside them closed and the woman engaged the lock.

She couldn't help but see Nick kneeling on the floor and know what they were doing. Shame burned through Miri, firing her cheeks, but another sensation fought for supremacy. It was the wild impulse to ignore the other woman's presence, and it was winning. Nick's passionate ministrations, continuing without pause, helped it along toward victory. With a sigh of defeat, she closed her eyes, struggled not to breathe too heavily and let his tongue work its magic.

The woman was in the process of washing her hands when the orgasm swept over Miri. Try as she did, she couldn't keep in a moan of satisfaction. Every muscle in her body quivered with release, and she slumped against Nick, who was still caressing her with slow strokes, coaxing every drop of pleasure from her.

The outer door closed, bringing Miri back to a semblance of awareness as Nick got to his feet. Her actions should shock her, and they did, but she was too limp with gratification to make an issue of what they had done.

He kissed her gently on the mouth before saying, "That was intense. There's a real wanton underneath that schoolmarm exterior, Miri."

"Only with you," she admitted, leaning against him with her arms on his shoulders. His hands moved between their bodies to free his cock from his jeans. Miri kept her head against his chest as he ripped open a foil packet taken from his pocket and covered his cock.

Her thighs parted wider when he shifted into position, aligning his cock with her pussy. With a soft gasp, Miri welcomed him fully inside. After the last orgasm, she didn't know if she could survive another, but he set about proving she could, using his cock and hands to stroke her to a fever pitch. As her pussy contracted around him, she tossed her head, biting hard on her tongue to hold in a cry.

Nick filled the silence with a groan as he came, pulling her so tightly against him that they were almost one person for a moment, especially when their heartbeats thundered in time with each other.

When it was over, he held her for a long moment before pressing a kiss to her neck. "Your place or mine?"

She was exhausted and opened her mouth to tell him she couldn't do this again tonight, needing time to recover, but her answer caught her by surprise. "Yours. I want to see where you live."

"It's your standard bachelor pad, but it has a bed."

"That's all we need."

AS HE'D SAID, HIS APARTMENT was standard fare—white walls, brown carpet and a single bedroom, which they didn't make it to. As soon as Nick closed the door, he swept Miri into his arms and carried her to the overstuffed leather sofa. She stretched out on the sumptuous cushions, supporting her head on an arm bent behind her. She smiled up at him as he stood over her. Her eyes focused on the bulge in his pants, and she licked her lips.

Nick settled onto the couch, straddling her, making his cock dig into her stomach. He braced his hands on either side of her head and leaned forward to kiss her. Miri opened her mouth when his lips touched hers, changing the kiss from casual to intense by sweeping her tongue inside his. She brought both hands forward to splay across his chest, pulling him closer.

Nick groaned when she sucked his lower lip into her mouth, and she grasped handfuls of his shirt to keep from vocalizing her own pleasure. Her pussy ached with need, despite the pleasure he'd already given her, and she arched her hips, finding no gratification in empty space.

Frustrated, Miri tore her mouth from Nick's before he could pin her tongue with his. "I want you." It was liberating to be so blunt with her emotions. So liberating, she tried it again. "I want your cock inside me."

Nick seemed surprised by her words but nodded. "Sure, darlin'. Whenever you're ready." He winked.

Miri couldn't hide a grin of satisfaction at his startled look when she shoved against his shoulders. He went tumbling off the couch, and she followed, now straddling him as they lay on the floor. She tugged at his T-shirt. "Now would be appreciated."

He groaned. "Can I have a minute to catch my breath? That was a helluva ride." "No, but it will be." She ignored his requests to take it easy as she pulled at his shirt until it was over his head. When he was bared from the waist up, she let her hands roam over his chest, raking her nails across his nipples. She enjoyed his sharp inhalation so much she scratched the tender nubs again.

"Damn." He didn't sound angry. Rather, surprise and something more colored his tone. Enjoyment, perhaps?

Miri bent her head so she could focus her attention on the button and zipper of his jeans. They yielded to her determined hands with a rasp, and she opened the pants to reveal her prize. Nick's underwear posed a slight deterrent, and she had to tug at the waistband of his jeans and briefs a few times until he cooperated by lifting his hips.

In her impatience, she got the pants no lower than his knees. Seated across his shins, she shifted slightly to maximize her mobility. Then Miri looked up at him, finding Nick watching her with amused indulgence. She wanted to wipe that expression off his face, wanted him to feel the same need she had, just as urgently. She hated being vulnerable, but if she was going to be, she refused to experience it alone.

"I'm going to fuck you now," she said, almost conversationally. He folded his hands behind his head. "Is that right?"

She nodded just once.

His grin held more than a small measure of self-satisfaction. "Wouldn't you be more comfortable on the bed?"

"I'll be plenty comfortable on your cock," she retorted.

A hearty laugh escaped him. "By all means, go for it. I'm not going to stop you." "No, you aren't." He still wasn't feeling the same urgency, but that was about to

change. Miri leaned forward, catching a brief glimpse of his stunned expression just before his face disappeared from her line of sight. He jumped when her lips touched the head of his cock, but she spared no mercy for him to adjust to the erotic intrusion. In a smooth motion, Miri engulfed his cock in her mouth, somehow accommodating all of him.

He tasted like come and latex, along with something uniquely him. It wasn't completely unpleasant, and she soon forgot her initial reaction to his flavor when his cock convulsed in her mouth. She began to suck, working her head up and down, and knew she had provoked the response she wanted when he started pumping his hips.

Miri had her hands braced on his thighs, but she brought up one to hold the base of his cock, squeezing lightly. Nick groaned when she moved her mouth in a circle around his shaft, applying more suction to the head.

His thrusts increased in speed, and he sounded hoarse when he spoke. "I'm about to come, darlin'. You're too good."

She bit him on the head, scraping her teeth across the sensitive flesh. When he uttered a wordless protest, she lifted her head to smile at him. "You aren't coming yet."

He growled, glaring at her. "Are you playing with me?"

Miri didn't respond verbally. Instead, she let her gaze settle on his cock while her hands dispensed with the tunic. Nick reached up to help with her bra, and she smacked his hand lightly. "This is my show, Nick."

He laughed, though it contained more strain than amusement. "I guess I'll just watch."

"For now." She unfastened the bra and tossed it onto the floor beside the tunic. Her sense of order winced at the mess, but desire overrode her natural prissiness, and she turned her attention to the jeans. Her hands shook with anticipation, making it slow work to strip her jeans and underwear down below her knees. Though they restrained her legs, she had no time to waste getting them off.

"Condoms?"

Nick pointed downward. "Right pocket of my jeans."

Miri reached behind her awkwardly, feeling for a bulge in the denim. When she found the pocket, she plunged her fingers inside and pulled out three condoms. With haste, she tore one off the roll. It resisted opening, so she used her teeth. Her urgent need was disquieting, but she was too immersed in it to back off, cool down and think about all the reasons why she shouldn't be attacking Nick—least of all, she wasn't like this. Clearly, she was when with Nick.

His cock jerked at her feathery touch when she rolled the condom down the shaft. Miri paused to caress his head, applying a small amount of pressure to the sensitive V until he lunged upward, his teeth clenched. Satisfied he finally felt the same driving desire as she did, she scooted higher up his body.

If not for the jeans hindering her legs, she could have been on him in seconds. It took close to a minute to position her pussy atop his cock and get a sense of balance. When she was centered, Miri sank down on him, and they both moaned when his cock filled her.

She dug her nails into his chest where she'd braced them and began arching up and down. "That feels so good." Miri circled her hips while clenching her pussy around his cock.

"You've got that right, darlin'. I could stay in your hot little pussy for hours."

A bead of sweat dripped into her eyes, but she didn't bother to wipe it away. "I can't wait that long."

"Me neither," he admitted with a grunt while driving forcefully inside her. His cock spasmed, making her womb quake in response. Miri was on the edge of coming, and when she scooted forward a smidge and arched her back, his cock rubbed right against her clit as she rode him. Their frantic thrusts pushed them closer to the edge, and she suddenly found herself falling over it.

The heat of his liquid satisfaction spread to her through the condom as he climaxed, and it triggered more convulsions in her pussy. She tightened her muscles around his cock and crested the peak of her orgasm, gradually slowing the speed of her thrusts until the last bit of tension faded, and she collapsed on top of him, breathless.

They didn't speak, and she was grateful not to have to make conversation. At that moment, she was still out of control, a sensation that terrified her. She needed time to gather her composure, which was impossible with his cock slowly waning inside her. After the way she had just behaved, she couldn't face him and act normally. It was better to hide her face against his chest and try to forget how wild she had been. That was easier to plan than execute with her body still glowing from the amazing release, and her inhabitations temporarily freed from restraint.

She knew, lying atop him, that she couldn't let this happen again. If he could make her lose control this way, she could easily end up like her mother. Miri couldn't allow herself to lose her hard-won self-respect on the altar of desire.

But when his cock hardened a few minutes later, and his hands cupped her breasts to rub her nipples, it never occurred to her to refuse him. In a matter of moments, she was swept away again, forgetting her previous resolutions.

Chapter Four

Nick waved off the last of the guys trying to talk him into going to the bar while dialing Miri's number. He hadn't seen her in the three days he had been on duty, hadn't even called her, but hadn't been able to think about anything except her during that time. The last two weeks of their affair had flown by, it seemed, and he still hadn't gotten enough of her.

It scared the hell out of him, but here he was, calling her after only three days of self-imposed silence, when he had been trying to make it a full week. Would she be happy to hear from him or irritated he had gone so long without speaking to her?

He grimaced as the phone rang, reminding himself she hadn't tried to call him at the station either, though it would have been a simple matter of looking up the number in the phone book. Perhaps she was managing to compartmentalize their casual fling better than he was.

She answered on the third ring, rasping, "Hello."

"Miri?"

"Yes. Nick?"

"You sound awful." He winced at his honesty.

"Thanks." She coughed before continuing. "I picked up a bug at school."

"I was going to bring by Chinese food, but maybe I'd better bring you soup instead." Smooth invitation. He shook his head at the way the words had emerged, leaving her little choice.

Silence filled the line for a moment. "I'm sick."

"I won't catch anything. Hearty New England stock, remember?" It was clear from her tone she was trying to get rid of him, so why wasn't he accepting that gracefully?

Again, she hesitated, finally saying, "I'm not feeling up to anything...if you know what I mean?"

His voice lowered, becoming more reassuring. "That's fine, darlin'. I'll bring food, DVDs, and pampering."

Her reluctance was evident, along with her weariness, when she spoke again. "Fine."

Nick didn't like the surge of relief that swept through him, nor the way his stomach clenched with anticipation at seeing her. He forced himself to sound neutral when replying. "Great. Do you want Chinese food or chicken soup?"

"Egg-drop soup sounds good."

"Right. I'll see you soon, darlin'." Nick hung up before she could retract her acquiescence, sensing she was on the verge of telling him not to come over. He didn't want to scrutinize too closely why he was so desperate to see her or why his experiment of imposing some distance between them had failed. Nor did he want to think about why he couldn't get her out of his mind or how it had hurt to know she thought he only wanted to come by for sex. It was a logical assumption on her part, since every date they'd been on had ended tangled in the sheets of one of their beds, so there was no reason for him to feel wounded.

No reason he wanted to examine anyway.

MIRI MADE LITTLE EFFORT with her appearance before Nick's arrival, deciding to let him see her complete with red nose, swollen eyes and an old robe left from college. This sudden move from casual sex into relationship realm alarmed her, maybe because she wanted to move to the next level as she never had before. When a man got too close, she'd had no trouble sending him on his way but didn't feel the same compulsion to do so with Nick.

Her insides had warmed in a disconcerting way when he'd said he was going to come by just to pamper her. No one had ever brought her soup or taken care of her when she was sick. It was disconcerting to have her casual lover showing such tender concern.

When the doorbell rang, the thoughts were still swirling through her mind as she tried to decide what was the best way to get rid of Nick and her own treacherous longings.

All thoughts of sending him on his way flew out of her brain when she opened the door to see Nick holding a large teddy bear under one arm and a bag of Chinese food in his hand. The bear held a heart that said "Get Well." Before she could school her reaction, she was reaching for the bear, cuddling it against her.

"You like it?" His boyish need to please was evident in his expression and the way he shifted from foot to foot.

Miri nodded, incapable of speech for a moment. Nick slipped past her to set the Chinese food and a bag of DVDs on the coffee table before turning back to take her in his arms.

Sick as she was, her body responded to his proximity, and it was strange to have him press a chaste kiss to her forehead instead of receiving the passionate greeting she had expected. Somehow, she ended up cuddled against him, with the bear forming an awkward barrier between them. Tears burned at the back of her eyes, and Miri blinked rapidly to dissolve them, not certain why she wanted to cry.

"C'mon. You should be resting." He guided her to the couch, seating her on the middle cushion. Looking sheepish, he touched the bear briefly. "Silly, huh?"

She shook her head. "It's wonderful." Her voice was wet with suppressed tears, but at that moment, she was unable to hide her emotions and hoped he would chalk it up to her illness. "Thank you."

Nick shrugged, as if trying to push aside his embarrassment. He didn't respond except to remove a Styrofoam container from the plastic bag and hand it to her. "Egg-drop soup." A plastic soup spoon followed before he arranged two boxes of food and chopsticks on the table.

Miri made a production of opening the soup and examining the contents before taking a small bite, desperate to avoid his eyes lest he see the vulnerability in hers. She only looked up when he called her name, jiggling two rental cases.

"I wasn't sure what you liked, so I picked up a chick flick and an action movie. Which will it be?"

She pointed to the action movie, in no mood to have her already-raw emotions exposed further by any heartrending issue the chick flick might explore. Nick put it in her DVD player before joining her on the couch.

As they watched the movie, eating, no words passed their lips. When Miri had eaten as much of the soup as she could, she put the lid on and leaned back against the cushion, carefully resting her head on his shoulder. Nick put aside his food to take her into his arms. A spark of electricity arced between them, but his demeanor was one of caretaker rather than lover as he held her.

She relaxed into him, enjoying his embrace more than she should. It was a foreign experience to have someone else care about her wellbeing, to take care of her. That it would be Nick, the man she was supposed to be having a fling with, made it even stranger. He wasn't supposed to be the sensitive type. All brawn with a massive dose of sex appeal—that was his persona. He wasn't supposed to upset her preconceived notions and make her start to fall for him.

Her eyes, drooping before, snapped open at the thought. Miri tensed, almost pulling away, as if she could escape her emotions just by putting some distance between them. Three days of silence on both of their parts hadn't done anything to diminish her desire for him, so why did she think withdrawing from his embrace would do anything?

"Miri? Are you okay?"

Slowly, she nodded, allowing her body to relax again. "I was falling asleep."

"Go ahead. I'll make sure you get to bed."

The words themselves were sexy but delivered in a nurturing manner. Miri tried to force her thoughts from her emotions to concentrate on the movie, but it was a long time before she was successful.

BY THE END OF THE MOVIE, Miri was snoring softly against him. Nick looked down at her upturned face, noting the lines of worry around her eyes, and wondered what haunted her.

She sighed in her sleep, snuggling closer. A glance at the clock revealed it was nearly ten, which meant he should get going. In other circumstances, he would have stayed with her for a few hours, but tonight, didn't feel the urge.

As he got to his feet, lifting her into his arms effortlessly, Nick acknowledged that wasn't true when his cock swelled against his jeans. He had the desire, but her needs outweighed his wants. Never before had he experienced this curious blend of tenderness and passion for a lover. Not one of the women he had been involved with in the past had ever evoked a need in him to take care of them.

Carrying her to her room, staring down at her, Nick faced an unpleasant truth. He was in love with Miri. It didn't give him the surge of terror he expected. Instead, as he placed her under the covers and brushed a kiss against her cheek, satisfying warmth spread through him, radiating from his heart, not his cock. For the life of him, he couldn't remember right then why he had fought so long against feeling something real for a woman.

"I love you," he said in a whisper, trying out the words, liking the way they sounded. Her eyes opened briefly. She locked gazes with him for just a second, before her eyes slammed closed again, and her snoring increased. It was just long enough for him to catch the glint of panic in her eyes.

Chapter Five

As soon as Miri opened her eyes the next morning, Nick's words swirled through the layers of her subconscious to lodge in the forefront of her mind. With a smothered groan, she rolled out of bed, desperate to escape her emotions. Panic was there, as it had been last night, but there was more. Was that giddy tickle in her chest happiness or simply the remnants of her cold?

Miri hurried into the bathroom, trying to deny she felt anything other than fear at Nick's confession. Her eyes revealed something different than her brain wanted to see. They were soft pools of darkness, tinged with a warm glow. Her lips tried to curve into a smile, and she had to school her expression into her most severe look, one usually reserved for recalcitrant students.

Dammit, she was pleased with Nick's words. Somehow, he had wormed his way into her life, burrowing into her heart in a way no man had ever done before. Her walls had dropped, her defenses had let her down...and she didn't care?

"I love you." Her lips formed the words hesitantly, and her voice was a rusty rasp in the enclosed space of the bathroom. She waited for some reaction, like the ceiling to fall on her, but nothing happened, other than a lightening in her chest.

Padding from the bathroom, forgetting about her morning ablutions, Miri continued practicing the words under her breath. Each time she said them, they came easier, until she almost thought she could say them to Nick when next they met.

HER FLEDGLING COMFORT with Nick's confession and her own response lasted until the next afternoon, when her phone rang. Not given to moments of intuition, it was with strange foreboding that Miri answered the telephone, every instinct screaming to ignore the out-of-area number. "Hello?"

"Miri, darling."

Her stomach churned as soon as her mother's voice came over the line. "Hello, Marnie." She'd used her given name since she was eight, when Marnie had decided she looked too young to have men know she had a daughter. "How are you?" To what did she owe the phone call? Marnie kept in touch infrequently, usually only if she wanted something, like money.

"Deliriously happy."

Ah, a new man. "Oh?"

"I'm getting married."

Miri's lips curled in a cynical grimace. "You're already married."

Marnie laughed. "Oh, darling, not for long."

"What happened with Herb?" Or was it Howard? After the number of uncles and stepfathers who had paraded through Miri's life, she couldn't keep them straight.

Her mother sighed, sounding impatient. "He's so boring. He doesn't understand me at all. Can you believe he wanted me to work with him? I can't think of anything duller than sitting in an office all day."

"So you went shopping for a new husband?"

Marnie's tone sharpened. "I didn't plan it. It just sort of happened, but I couldn't stop how I felt. Craig is the one."

"Hmm."

Not picking up on Miri's skepticism, Marnie continued. "He's never been married, has no children, owns a chain of restaurants and has the most beautiful yacht. We're going to spend six months sailing around the world for our honeymoon. It's a ninety-footer, complete with a full staff—"

Miri tuned out her mother's enthusiastic description of the yacht and other material goods. It was just another match made in material heaven. One thing she could credit to her mother was Marnie's ability to trade up. She could certainly pick her targets. The thought of using men so callously turned Miri's stomach, though she had little sympathy for the men who had married her mother. They should have realized what they were getting into. Loving Marnie was no excuse to be blind to her faults.

Nothing good ever came from love. It was a lesson Miri had learned repeatedly over the years, but a moment of weakness had nearly undermined her. Whatever fragile emotional attachment she had almost allowed to grow had to be firmly squashed. Her mother's phone call and latest marriage was a timely reminder of what Miri had known most of her life. She was better off alone than allowing herself to love anyone as passionately as she could love Nick. She would lose herself in him, and for what? An emotion that couldn't possibly last. She had to protect herself, and that meant hardening her heart.

NICK POUNDED ON MIRI'S door relentlessly, knowing she was home. He had seen her car in the garage when he peeked in the window. Her avoidance of him the past five days was about to end. He was going to force a confrontation, damn her wishes and his own fear of rejection. Limbo was worse than knowing how she felt about him, even if her feelings weren't mutual.

Finally, she opened the door, a trace of annoyance in her expression. "Nick? What's so urgent?"

He didn't wait for an invitation, pushing past her. She followed him, emanating arctic silence as he turned to face her in the living room. "Why have you been avoiding me?"

Miri frowned, giving every appearance of ignorance. "I don't know what you mean.

I missed three days of school and have been struggling to catch up with everything."

"You haven't had time to return even one of my calls in the last five days?" He snorted. "Yeah."

"I had other priorities."

Her cool façade, such a contrast to the inferno burning inside him, was infuriating. He took a step closer, absurdly pleased by the way she stood her ground, though he wouldn't have minded some acknowledgement she wasn't as unaffected as she pretended. "Liar."

Her eyes widened. "Excuse me?"

"You're running scared." Nick shook his head. "It won't work. You have to face me sometime."

Miri turned partially away from him. "I have no idea what you're talking about."

He touched her shoulder, and she tensed at the light contact. "I know you heard me."

She shrugged him off. "Heard what?"

He pressed her back against his chest. "I told you I loved you."

Miri shook her head. "No."

"I did." He turned her resisting body so she was facing him, though she avoided his gaze. Nick lifted her chin, forcing her to look into his eyes. "I do. I love you."

Fear flared in her eyes. "You're crazy. You don't know me."

"I know all I need to."

She pulled away. "No, you don't. You don't know anything important about me. Did you know my mother has been married seven times...about to be eight? There was also a countless parade of uncles in my life, always a priority over me." Tears leaked from the corners of her eyes, and she brushed them away with an impatient gesture. "Do you want to know how many of them had grabby hands? How many times she ignored me when I told her?"

His stomach clenched with anger. "Give me their names. They'll never hurt you again."

She shook her head. "None of them ever really hurt me, not nearly as much as knowing my mother needed a man—any man—more than she needed to live up to her responsibility to me."

Nick reached for her, not allowing her to shove away his hands. He pulled her stiff body into his arms. "I'm sorry you had to go through that."

"It doesn't matter now. It taught me an important lesson. I don't want to love a man, and I don't want one to love me." Her expression was a perfect sheet of ice when she looked up at him. "I don't want your love, Nick. You're wasting your time trying to convince me."

He shook his head, refusing to believe. "You don't mean that. It's natural to be frightened after the experiences in your childhood, but I wouldn't hurt you."

"I know, because you'll never have the chance." Miri withdrew from him, pointing to the door. "You need to leave now."

"Miri—"

"Go. I don't want to see you again."

Nick stared at her for half a minute, searching for a crack in her veneer but finding none. His shoulders slumped, and he took a step toward the door. "You'll change your mind. You just need time to think things through."

Miri turned away from him. "I won't. I don't want you, and I definitely don't love you."

He winced at the pain her words caused. Nick had the fleeting urge to rage at her, but it faded quickly. Nothing he could say would reach her right then, emotionally frozen as she was. He could only hope she might come to her senses and open up to him in the coming days. His happiness—and hers—depended on it. He walked away without looking back, not wanting her to see the tears misting his eyes, wondering if she was as close to weeping as he was. In her frigid state, he doubted it.

Chapter Six

M iri poured a cup of coffee, deliberately avoiding the gaze of Janine, the French teacher, the closest thing she had to a best friend. She hoped Janine wouldn't look up from the TV when she slid into a seat at the table in the staff room.

"Finally, a minute alone." Janine turned from the TV, giving Miri an assessing glance. "Spill."

Assuming a cool expression, Miri looked up from the newspaper spread across the table. "What?"

"Something's up with you. A man?" "No."

Janine laughed. "Yeah, sure. Only a man can make you as testy and disagreeable as you've been lately."

Frowning, Miri met her Janine's eyes. "I don't know what you're talking about." "I'm talking about that delicious firefighter you were banging for a short time. Suddenly, you no longer say a thing about him, and you're a regular grouch. Clearly, a lack of sex is to blame."

"Well, aren't you full of insights today?" Miri glared at her.

Janine nodded, asking matter-of-factly, "Did he dump you?"

Miri inched up her chin. "No. As a matter of fact, he's madly in love with me." Why bother with the pretense? Janine was the only person who had even an inkling of how her childhood had been, so she would be the only one who could understand why Miri had rejected Nick.

Her green eyes sparkled with excitement. "That's fabulous. Are you keeping it hush-hush until you have a firm commitment?"

"No. I broke it off."

"What?" Janine's outburst carried throughout the room, briefly rousing the interest of Gertrude, the gym teacher, before she returned to a thick manual of physiology. "Are you out of your mind? You finally find a man worth keeping and you discard him?"

Miri drew into herself, wrapping her hands around the coffee mug to draw some warmth from it, upon finding none from her so-called friend. "You know I don't want a man, not long-term anyway."

Janine's voice lowered to a whisper when she leaned across the table, coming closer. "You aren't going to turn into your mother by daring to have a relationship, Miri. You don't really want to be alone for the rest of your life, do you? If so, it's a very bleak future you're contemplating."

She got to her feet, abandoning the coffee. "I'm happy as I am. I didn't ask for your opinion, and I'd appreciate you keeping it to yourself." Without allowing Janine the opportunity to respond, Miri swept from the staff room, refusing to look back or acknowledge the icy ball in her stomach that had formed at Janine's words. No, it wouldn't be bleak to be alone. It would be safe and predictable. No one could hurt her as long as she kept them all at arms' length. She regretted the friendship she had allowed to blossom with Janine and vowed it would end right then.

IN KEEPING WITH HER decision, she met Janine with a chill tone when the other woman stopped by her classroom a little after four. "Yes?"

"I need to tell you something—"

"I accept your apology." She stuffed papers into her eel-skin briefcase, keeping her profile turned from Janine.

"I'm not here to apologize."

Her distraught tone finally caught Miri's attention, forcing her to look up. "What's wrong?"

"There's been a fire at the country club...the roof collapsed." Janine's eyes were wide with apprehension, and her hands trembled when she reached out to Miri. "Two firefighters were killed, and three more have been taken to the hospital."

"Nick." Was he working a thirty-six-hour shift this week, or was it one of his three days off? She didn't know. Miri didn't question her reaction as she dropped her briefcase and scooped up her purse, fishing for car keys as she ran to the door. Janine shouted something behind her, but she didn't take time to figure out what it was as she ran through the building to the parking lot. She had to get to Nick. Please let him be alive.

THE HALLS AT POPLIN Hills General were crowded with friends and family members of the firefighters, making it difficult for Miri to push her way through the throng to the front desk. Three nurses engaged in various tasks ignored her for a long moment until she thumped her hand onto the counter to get their attention.

The oldest one looked up from her paperwork. "May I help you?"

"I'm here...is Nick..." She took a deep breath, struggling to compose herself so she could force out the question, almost afraid to hear the answer. "Is Nick Martin here?"

The nurse glanced at a clipboard before looking up. "He's in room 115."

Miri turned from the desk, heading down the hallway.

"Miss, you can't go back there. Only family—"

She broke into a jog, hoping to outrun the nurse's admonishment and make it to the room before anyone stopped her. The woman's voice faded the farther away Miri moved from the desk, and she dared to hope she would make it to the room.

She passed 113 and 114 before seeing a man in a blue security uniform moving toward her from the opposite end of the hall. Miri increased her pace and pushed her way into 115 as security called to her.

Her breath caught in her throat when she saw the body lying in the bed, wrapped in bandages from almost head to foot. His leg was suspended in traction, and what visible skin there was around the bandages bore blisters. She walked forward, bracing herself. The person lying there was in bad shape.

"Nick." His name was a choked whisper, and she sagged forward, wanting to touch him but afraid of hurting him. "Oh, Nick, what have I done?"

"Miri?"

She jerked with shock at his voice, spinning around to find Nick standing behind her. Her mouth dropped open, and she drank in the sight of him, noticing the bandages on his arm and across his forehead. She threw herself into his arms. "You're alive."

He held her close. "I wasn't inside when the roof collapsed. I got my injuries going in with the second squad to help get out my buddies."

Sobs shook her body, and she clutched his shirt. "I thought you were dying or dead. I was such an idiot." Miri raised her head. "I could have lost you, and you never would have known—"

The door opened, admitting the guard. "You can't be in here." Nick waved his hand. "We'll leave in just a second."

Miri turned her head in time to see the guard's stern expression fade. "Never mind. I didn't realize she was with you, Nick." He turned to the door, leaving a heavy silence in his wake.

Finally, Nick cleared his voice. "You were saying?"

She hesitated, finding her courage had deserted her at the penultimate moment. During the frantic drive to the hospital, all she could think about was how could she go on without Nick, but now that he was safe, she found it impossible to remove the last fragment of the wall protecting her heart. Instead, she asked, "Who is the man in the bed?"

"My chief, Brady Holland. I'm waiting with him until his wife arrives. She works in Portland."

"Will he make it?"

Nick sighed. "We don't know yet."

Still clutching his shirt, Miri looked up at him. "What you do is dangerous."

He nodded. "Yes. I love it, but I'd give it up if you ask me to. I finally understand how my brother could walk away from his career for his wife."

Tears trickled from her eyes, and she buried her face against his chest. "I couldn't ask that of you."

He pushed up her chin, forcing her to meet his eyes. "Haven't you figured out by now I'll do anything for you? I love you, Miri, more than I've ever loved being a firefighter. More than I've ever loved anything. I want to spend my life making you happy, if you'll let me."

The wall crumbled with what she swore was an audible crack. Miri's muscles refused to support her, and she slumped against him, letting his T-shirt absorb her tears. "I love you, Nick." The words were strange on her tongue, but she meant them with every ounce of her being. When she dared to look up, she found Nick's lips trembling and couldn't tell if his eyes were glazed with tears or if the mist was from hers. "I love you." This time, the words were easier to say. "I don't know how it happened or when, but I do love you. Can you forgive me for pushing you away?"

"It doesn't matter what happened in the past." His words carried significant meaning, not just for their history but also for her own. "All that matters is the future."

She stretched on her tiptoes to kiss him, finding herself optimistic about the future for the first time ever. With the thawing of her heart, she was free to imagine a dizzying array of possibilities in their future, and none were bleak. How could they be with Nick by her side?

Bonus Excerpt

If you enjoyed "Ablaze," you might also like "A Royal Pain."

Harper Gaines silenced her cellphone when it vibrated in her scrubs pocket before getting back to the lance corporal, whose leg she was currently bending. "Just like that. And out. Don't forget to exhale." She guided him through the exercise twice more before stepping back slightly to have him perform the rest himself. He was making great progress, and she was certain he'd be released from the VA Hospital for this particular injury in a matter of weeks.

Her phone buzzed again, and she took it discreetly from her pants. Her eyes widened, and she smiled her pleasure as she brought it to her ear, turning slightly to shield her conversation while still allowing a view of the Marine's form. "Tucker Carlton, I haven't heard from you in months."

His voice sounded like he was standing right next to her, though he was probably still in Montrovia, where he was the royal family's personal physician. "It's been a madhouse since Bennet...Prince Bennet crashed his racecar. Did you hear about that?"

"Of course." Even in America, it was big news when a member of a royal family almost died, especially if it was due to some daredevil sport like racing. "How is your patient?"

"Maddening." His cheerful tone belied his words. "He's also managed to chase off the second physical therapist just this morning. That's two in three weeks."

"Impressive." When the Marine looked up, she gave him a smile before turning a slight bit more from him. "He sounds like a spoiled brat."

Tucker hesitated. "Oh, he can be, but he's a good person too. I'm looking for a resilient physical therapist, who can take his crap and give it right back. Do you know anyone who might be interested in the position?"

Harper frowned as she ran through a mental list of colleagues. "Um, maybe. I have some contacts—"

He interrupted her with a laugh. "I'm talking about you, sweetheart. Are you up for the task?"

Her eyes widened, and she saw the shock in her expression in the full-wall mirror she was partially facing. "Me? But I have a job."

"And some vacation time, right? And if you tell your boss where you're going, I'm sure he'd let you take a leave of absence for this assignment. Gotta be good press to have a VA physical therapist get a prince of the Casparian House of Montrovia walking again."

It was tempting, but she hesitated. "I have patients..."

"Would you like to hear the salary?" Without waiting for an answer, he named a sum that made her eyes cross. "That's just until he's up and moving again, so it could be a few weeks."

"Or months or years. Level with me. Does his injury keep him from being able to walk? Because if it does, I won't beat a dead horse. He'll have to accept his limitations and focus on performing the tasks that will help him live as a quadriplegic." She couldn't in good conscience take the position with the prince expecting more than she could deliver, even if the payment was enough to completely pay off her remaining student loans.

"Paraplegic," said Tucker, his voice all business now. "He was initially paralyzed from mid-chest downward, but the corticosteroids and surgery relieved some of the compression. He's stabilized for now with little sensation below his mid-thigh."

"Can he walk again?"

Tucker hesitated. "I believe he can, but I'd like your professional opinion. Are you up for an assessment?"

"I'm hardly flying all the way to Strater for an assessment. If I come, it's to work."

His grin was obvious in his tone. "I figured, and the capital city is Stratta, not Strater. Can I persuade you?"

Harper held back for a moment before curiosity overwhelmed her. "I think you can, as long as I can arrange a leave-of-absence."

"Excellent. Let me know as soon as you have a firm decision, and I'll ask the king's assistant to arrange your travel. I'm sure Fiona Claremont will be thrilled to have another American sullying up the palace." He laughed as he finished speaking.

"She sounds charming."

"Oh, not as charming as Bennet." He was downright chortling now.

Harper frowned. "You're making me second-guess my decision, Tuck."

"Don't do that, Harp. You won't regret it, but I won't sugarcoat it either. You have your work ahead of you."

She squared her shoulders, catching sight of the resolve in her expression, framed by the short black pixie cut, which emphasized the creaminess of her complexion. "We'd best get started as soon as possible then."

Optimism spread through her as she hung up and finished the session with the lance corporal. After that, she cleared a leave with her boss—who was just as happy to accommodate as Tucker had speculated—and had a whirlwind schedule faxed to her home by the time she arrived that evening. Smiling down at the itinerary in front of her, she was confident in her decision.

MAYBE THAT CONFIDENCE had come too soon. She was forced to consider the idea as she gazed around her when stepping foot into the summer palace of the royal family, where they were currently in residence. It was luxurious beyond compare, and enough to really underscore to her how out-of-place she was with her Midwestern, middleclass upbringing when contrasted with her surroundings.

Firming her shoulders, she reminded herself she was there for her expertise in physical therapy, and because she wasn't afraid of a challenge. This might be outside her comfort zone, but she couldn't let that hold her back.

By the time she recognized a familiar face a few moments later, she was feeling more certain again. She walked forward to meet Tucker, who was beaming at her. His dark skin had gotten a couple of shades darker, and his curls, neatly cropped close to his head last time she'd seen him, had grown out into a two-inch high start of an Afro. He looked tired, but also fantastic.

The abrasive sound of a throat clearing broke apart their hug of greeting, and she smoothed down her slacks and shirt before turning to face the source. Somehow, she kept a pleasant smile on her lips even as she faced the expression of disapproval directed her way. The owner of the expression was a tall, sour-looking brunette with a furrow in her brow that looked like it was there perpetually. Right away, she was certain it was the Fiona Claremont Tucker had mentioned to her.

"Now that you're here, I'll show you to the servants' quarters. The driver will have already sent in your bags. After that, the doctor will want you to meet the prince, I'm sure. Once that's finished, I have a list of rules to discuss with you."

Harper firmed her spine and took a step closer. She extended her hand as she said, "Hello. You must be Ms. Claremont. Thank you for making the travel arrangements." For a moment, her hand remained there with no sign of acknowledgement.

Eventually, Fiona made a production of juggling the items in her hands to take her hand in a limp-fish squeeze before quickly releasing it. "Of course, Ms. Gaines. It's my job to help the royal family, and the doctor seems to think you might provide some assistance to Prince Bennet."

There was a chill in the air, and Harper briefly wondered if Tucker and Fiona had a thing—or had once had a thing, and the woman was jealous of the history between them. Once the other woman cast a frigid, dismissive glance at Tucker, she quickly revised that hypothesis. Whatever Fiona's problem, it wasn't because she was involved with Tucker, or because Harper had once dated him.

It didn't take long for Fiona to show her to a room three floors up. It was toward the back of the palatial home, and when she left her at the door, she parted with a crisp, "Next time you enter, please use the servants' entrance instead of the main entryway, Ms. Gaines."

Before Harper could acknowledge the admonishment, or even think about telling her the driver had dropped her at the main entrance, the other woman was gone in a cloud of expensive perfume and surrounded by an invisible, impenetrable icy shield. With a shrug, she watched her leave before entering her room.

It wasn't as opulent as everything else she'd seen, but it was a room reserved for servants. Everything was rather spartan, but all clean and of obviously excellent quality. She was certain the bedframe, though plain, was an antique by the patina on the wood. The armoire and dresser were the same. There was nothing about which to complain—not that she would have anyway. It would have started off her employment on the wrong foot, and she was certain Fiona wouldn't have cared if she was sleeping on a bed of nails. She gave off that kind of vibe.

It had been a long flight, though hardly a burden on the private jet they had arranged for her. She'd felt almost guilty wasting all those resources for just herself, but hadn't exactly minded having the whole space to herself without having to share idle conversation with strangers. Still, she hadn't been able to sleep no matter how she'd tried, and she was starting to feel the effects of not sleeping for almost ten hours.

She pushed aside her exhaustion, going into the bathroom that appeared to connect to another door that was currently unlocked, and splashed water on her face. Her makeup was nonexistent by that point, but she didn't bother adding more. It was too much effort.

When she stepped out of her room a few minutes later, she was unsurprised to find Tucker waiting for her. She smiled at him and wove her arm through his, allowing him to take a bit of her weight as he led her down the hallway.

"Frigid Fiona put you in the middle of nowhere, didn't she?"

She shrugged. "I don't know. Probably. Where are you?"

"I'm in a room next to Bennet's, in his wing of the house, but Frigid Fiona hates that. She likes to remind me every chance she gets that I'm an employee, not a guest, and certainly not worthy of a suite." He laughed.

"She's as charming as I expected."

He shrugged. "Let's see if I did Bennet justice in describing him."

Harper swallowed down a bit of nervousness. "Yeah, okay." By the time they made the long trek to the prince's wing, she'd had plenty of time to quell her nerves.

They still flared to life again when Tucker knocked on one of two French doors before entering. She followed him inside, looking around surreptitiously and trying not to ogle the blatant display of wealth.

"Bennet, where are you, man?" asked Tucker.

"In here," called a deep voice with a crisp accent. It wasn't quite English-sounding, but similar.

From the research she'd done before coming to Montrovia, she knew the small island country had been founded when Mad George the Third banished his ill-liked distant relation there and ordered him imprisoned. At some point, the imprisonment had turned to a governorship during the Regent's reign, and Montrovia had been an independent monarchy for the last hundred-plus years after a brief, nearly bloodless war with England. Their rich oil deposits and rare Earth minerals had probably had something to do with England's acquiescence.

She held her breath as the prince came into sight, battling the latest surge of nerves. Her first sight of him wasn't the professional evaluation it should be. Instead, she noticed his lean, toned physique displayed by the tight white tank top he wore. It wasn't what she would've expected from a Prince, but she couldn't argue that it certainly highlighted how muscular his arms were—which reminded her that she was there to work, not ogle the Prince.

This time, when she ran her gaze down his body, it was more professional as she assessed his strengths. It was good that he had strong arms, because he needed that to lift himself in and out of the chair and to be able to move it on his own. She was pleased to see it was a manual wheelchair, instead of a power chair, which would have reduced his need to exercise and might have made his recovery that much slower. Either Tucker or one of the physical therapists must have been responsible for that choice, because she doubted the hospital and convalescent homes where he had spent his first few weeks would have tried to persuade him to go with the manual chair if he'd insisted on a power one.

Summoning a deep breath and a smile, she moved her gaze from his body to his face, muscles immediately tightening at the smug expression he wore. Her smile felt strained under the prince's gaze. She caught her breath slightly at the odd coloring, somewhere between purple and blue, and fringed by long brown eyelashes. His face was symmetrical perfection, as though carved by a skilled sculptor, and his cheekbones looked sharp enough to cut any finger that dared wander down it. She might've been overwhelmed by his appearance if not for the faint curl of his lips and the complete disinterest in his gaze.

Tucker stepped forward, putting a casual hand on her midback as he urged her forward. "This is the new physical therapist I told you about, Bennet. Harper Gaines, meet Prince Bennet Casparian."

She held out her hand, realizing after extending it that he had no intention of reciprocating. She let it hang awkwardly for a moment before dropping it back to her side. She was still nervous, but was quickly becoming familiar with another emotion—annoyance.

"You did that wrong, Tucker. You're supposed to introduce the prince to the commoner first, not the other way around." His voice was a rich baritone, and his accent was not quite English, but still even more alluring in its uniqueness. It was too bad he apparently only used it to deliver scathing comments.

Tucker shrugged. "Royal decorum isn't my thing, Bennet."

The prince didn't reply to Tucker's comment. Instead, his gaze hardened as he looked up at Harper after letting his gaze sweep over her form in a similar fashion to the one she'd used to appraise him. When he met her eyes, he gave her a lazy smile. "You're younger than I expected, and prettier too. You should consider makeup and doing something with your hair."

She squeezed her hands into fists as she took a deep breath while reminding herself this might be the prince's coping mechanism. Even if it wasn't, and she had to deal with that sort of attitude every day, she could do it. She'd had difficult patients before, and she had come expecting an adversarial relationship with the prince, at least in the beginning. "You aren't what I expected either, Your Highness."

He cocked a brow. "How so?"

She just shrugged, not wanting to get into a discussion of the importance of manners. "If you're ready, I'd like to do an assessment."

He stiffened slightly. "What does that entail?"

She arched a brow. "Did neither one of your previous physical therapists ask for an assessment?"

His expression darkened. "The hideous dragon lady from Belgium attempted such a thing, but I refused to cooperate. The simpering miss from Stratta seemed to use it as an excuse to fondle the royal prince."

She resisted the urge to loudly assure him she wouldn't do such a thing. Instead, she managed a smile and asked sweetly, "Would you please consent, Prince Bennet? I need to know where you are so I can figure out the best way to help you reach your maximum potential."

He stiffened again, his expression completely closed off. "There's nothing you can do to help me."

"Won't you at least give me a chance to try?" She squared her shoulders. "I'm very good at what I do."

He made a scoffing sound. "How old are you? You look like you've barely finished college."

"I'm twenty-seven," she said in an even tone. "I'm a fully qualified physical therapist, and I've helped a lot of clients. Even those who don't want to be helped, and who were very stubborn about the whole situation." She bit her tongue as she uttered the indiscreet words, but couldn't call them back.

He glared up at her. "I don't like your tone, or your attitude. Send her home, Tucker."

"No," said Tucker and Harper simultaneously.

Find at your favorite vendor[1] or buy directly from my website[2].

---

1. https://www.books2read.com/u/3k0vvW

2. http://kittunstall.com/downloads/arp/

About Kit Kyndall

Kit Kyndall is the pen name *USA Today* bestselling author Kit Tunstall uses when writing contemporary erotic romances. It's simply a way to separate the myriad types of stories she writes so readers know what to expect with each "author."

Join Kit's Mailing List[1] **to keep up with new releases and receive exclusive content.**

---

1. http://eepurl.com/bpdvb9

Also by Kit Kyndall

Kingwood Prep
Catching His Eye

Protectors
Safe Harbor
Hart & Soal

Sage Valley
Reunion
A Second Chance

SpicyShorts
Pawn
Two Cowboys for Cady
Ebony Enigma
Wrong Groom
Model Behavior
Biology Lessons

Mai Tais on the Beach
All Grown Up
SpicyShorts Bundle

Well...
Well-Seasoned

Standalone
Playing His Game
Snowbound
Student Bodies
Double Delights
Tied To You
Seduction
A Royal Pain
Ablaze
The Island
Submission
Falling For The Warrens
Out Of Bounds